© 1991 Twin Books Corp.

This 1991 edition published by Derrydale Books,
distributed by Outlet Book Company, Inc.,
A Random House Company
225 Park Avenue South
New York, NY 10003

Directed by HELENA Productions Ltd.
Illustrated by Van Gool-Lefevre-Loiseaux

Produced by Twin Books
15 Sherwood Place
Greenwich, CT 06830
Printed and bound in Spain

ISBN 0-517-05421-3

8 7 6 5 4 3 2 1

Tom Thumb

Van Gool

Twin Books

DERRYDALE BOOKS
New York

Once upon a time, there lived two peasants in a little hut in the woods. Although they were poor, they were very happy. However, there was one thing they yearned for. This was not gold or diamonds. They both wanted a child.

"I would be happy with only one child," said the husband.

"So would I," said his wife. "Even if the child were no bigger than my thumb."

In time, they did have a child—a beautiful little boy. He was blond and sweet, but very, very small. In fact, he was no bigger than a thumb. So the peasant and his wife named the child Tom Thumb.

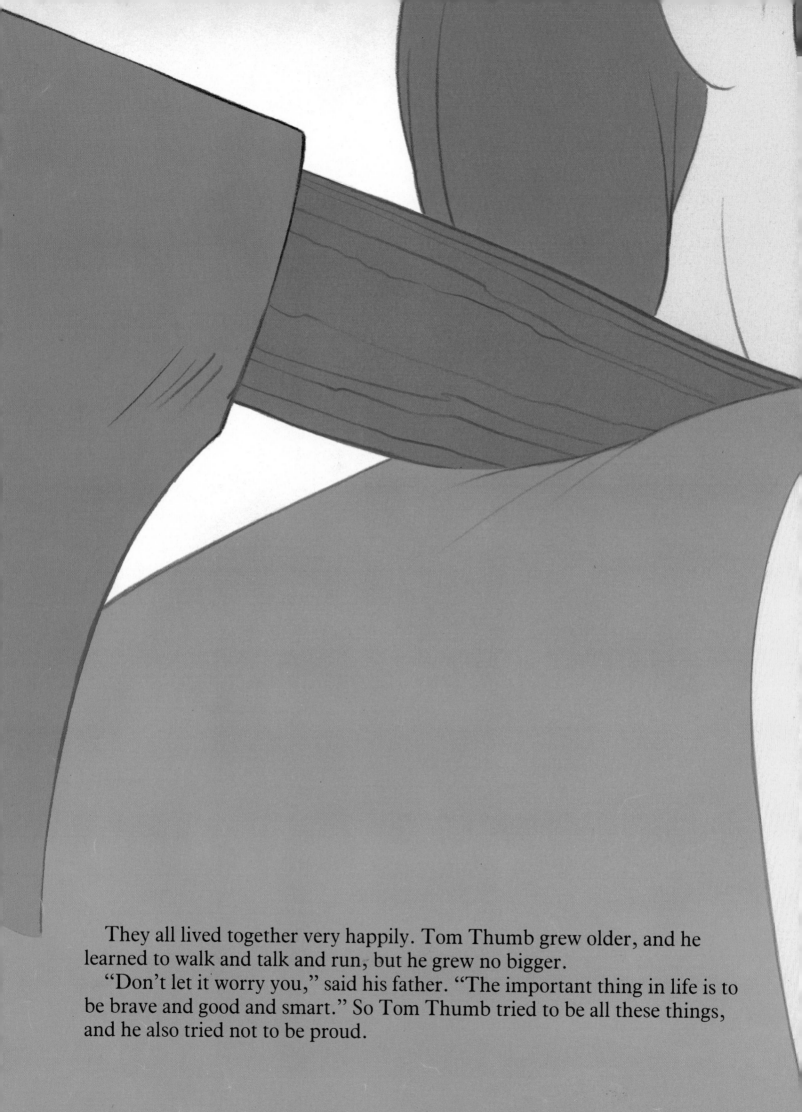

They all lived together very happily. Tom Thumb grew older, and he learned to walk and talk and run, but he grew no bigger.

"Don't let it worry you," said his father. "The important thing in life is to be brave and good and smart." So Tom Thumb tried to be all these things, and he also tried not to be proud.

In spite of his small size, Tom was a great help to his father on the farm. When his father was plowing or hitched the horse to go to market, Tom Thumb would sit on the horse's bridle, calling commands, and the gentle horse would obey.

One day, two strangers were passing by, and saw the horse being driven by Tom Thumb. One of them thought, "We would make a fortune if we sold this little fellow to the circus. People would be astonished that one so small could command a great animal like a horse, or even an elephant."

"Let us find his father," said the other.

The two men told Tom Thumb's father that they wished to hire him to work on their farm. And they offered him a heavy moneybag.

"I would be a monster if I sold my child," said the father. "But Papa," said Tom Thumb, "you need the money, and I would like to have the adventure. When I have worked out my time, I will come home."

So his father took the heavy moneybag and Tom Thumb rode away with the two men.

While they were walking along, Tom Thumb heard the two men discussing their plans.

"We will sell him to the circus, for a lot of money. And since the bag I gave his father was really filled with stones, we will do very well," said the man on whose hat Tom was perched.

When Tom realized they had cheated his father, he decided to run away at the first opportunity. That evening they stopped for the night, and the men put Tom Thumb on the ground while they made a fire.

Without waiting a moment, Tom Thumb scuttled into the undergrowth and hid himself under the leaves of a fern. The two scoundrels searched and called to him, but he didn't answer. When they searched the opposite side of the camp, Tom Thumb quietly hurried away.

Night had fallen, and Tom was miles from home.
"I will find my way back tomorrow," he said.
"Tonight I will stay here." And he curled up and
slept under a mushroom.

The next morning, Tom woke early and started the long walk home. Sometime later, he met two young thieves who were looking for a rich man's house to rob. Tom Thumb decided to take advantage of them and said, "I know where the rich miller lives in the next village. If you take me there, I will show you how to get into his house."

The thieves were easily fooled and they took Tom Thumb to the village, which was not far from his house. He showed the thieves a way into the miller's house. Then Tom scrambled up to the window and escaped, calling out, "Thieves! Thieves!" to the villagers. The two were captured, and Tom Thumb was almost home.

Growing tired, Tom stopped to rest in a nearby barn. It was filled with golden, sweet-smelling hay, and he decided to take a nap before resuming his journey. While he slept, snuggled in the hay, he dreamt of being home with his mother, who was singing lullabies to him.

Tom was so fast asleep that he did not awaken
when the farmer's wife came into the barn. In
putting a forkful of hay into the cow's manger, she
put him into the manger, too!

Tom Thumb awoke as the cow took a great mouthful of the hay in which he was sleeping. Suddenly, he found himself in the cow's mouth, trying to avoid her great teeth as they ground the hay! When the cow opened her mouth to take another bite, Tom Thumb jumped back into the manger. But he wasn't safe yet, for the cow continued to eat the hay, and with each bite, she came closer.

Really frightened, Tom cried out, "Help, help!"
The farmer's wife heard a voice that seemed to come
from the cow's head and thought it was the cow
calling! Terrified, she ran for help.

She came back with the mayor, who also heard the voice calling and thought it was the cow.

"This animal is bewitched," he said. "Take it into the far pasture and leave it there until the spell is broken."

The farmer's wife took the cow
to the pasture at the edge of the
village, unaware that Tom Thumb
rode along by the cow's ear.

Meanwhile, an old grey wolf was
watching from a nearby wood. He
decided that the cow would make a
good dinner. As the wolf drew
closer and closer, the poor cow
became very frightened. But just as
the wolf was about to attack her,
Tom Thumb jumped off the cow's
head and onto the wolf.

"Great wolf," said Tom Thumb, "you don't want to eat this skinny old cow. I know where you can get plenty of food—good food, like sausages. If you carry me to the next village, you can go and eat there as often as you like without anyone being the wiser."

The wolf was surprised, but he thought, "Many meals in peace are better than one cow now." So he agreed to take Tom Thumb to the next village.

It was midnight when they reached the village. "It is the third house after the little bridge," Tom told the wolf. "And there is a window you can crawl through at the back of the house that leads to a cellar."

The wolf crept into the cellar and soon found himself in the pantry. The table was covered with food—sausages, bacon, ham, and more. The wolf ate all he could hold.

At last he thought it was time to leave, but he had eaten so much, he was too fat to squeeze through the window. When Tom Thumb saw that the wolf was truly stuck, he called out as loud as he could:

"Papa! Mama! Help me! Help me!
The wolf is trapped in the cellar!"

It was his own house that Tom had brought the wolf to! When his father heard the voice of his son calling, he picked up a great carving knife in the kitchen and ran down the cellar stairs. But the sound of heavy footsteps scared the wolf so much that he managed to wiggle through the window and was gone.

It was a happy reunion. Tom Thumb was home—a bit bruised and bedraggled, tired and hungry, but eager to tell his parents all about his adventures.

"It wasn't easy to escape the scoundrels, the thieves, the cow, and the wolf," he concluded. "But I did, and now I'm home to stay."

That night, Tom Thumb was back in his own bed in his own house at last. As he went to sleep he thought about his adventures, and said to himself, "Papa was right. The important thing in life is not to be grand or to have money. The important thing is to be brave and good and smart." And then he fell into a well-earned sleep.